Series consultant: Dr Terry Jennings

Designed by Jane Tassie

The authors and publisher would like to thank Sam, Samantha and the staff and pupils of the Charles Dickens J & I School, London, and everyone at the London Glassblowing Centre for their help in making this book. Photograph on p18 kindly supplied by Halls Garden Products Limited.

A CIP record for this book is available from the British Library.

ISBN 0-7136-6193-3

First paperback edition published 2002
First published 1999 by A & C Black Publishers Limited
37 Soho Square, London W1D 3QZ
www.acblack.com

Text copyright
© 1999 Nicola Edwards and Jane Harris
Photographs copyright
© 1999 Julian Cornish-Trestrail

Typeset in 23/28pt Gill Sans Infant and 25/27 pt Soupbone Regular

Printed in Singapore by Tien Wah Press (Pte.) Ltd

A & C Black uses paper produced with elemental chlorine-free pulp, harvested from managed sustainable forests.

Safety note: children working on the activities featured in this book should be made aware of the dangers of broken glass and of the importance of careful handling of glass objects.

Science Explorers

Glass

Exploring the science
of everyday materials

Nicola Edwards and
Jane Harris

Photographs by
Julian Cornish-Trestrail

A & C Black · London

Glass is made in a factory.
Lots of things are made
of glass.

We've collected
all these!

This special, tough
piece of glass is
like a window.

I can see
right through it.

4

The walls of this building are made of glass. The glass lets a lot of light through.

This paperweight is made of thick glass. It feels heavy.

Look at this glass vase.
The sides are
so delicate.

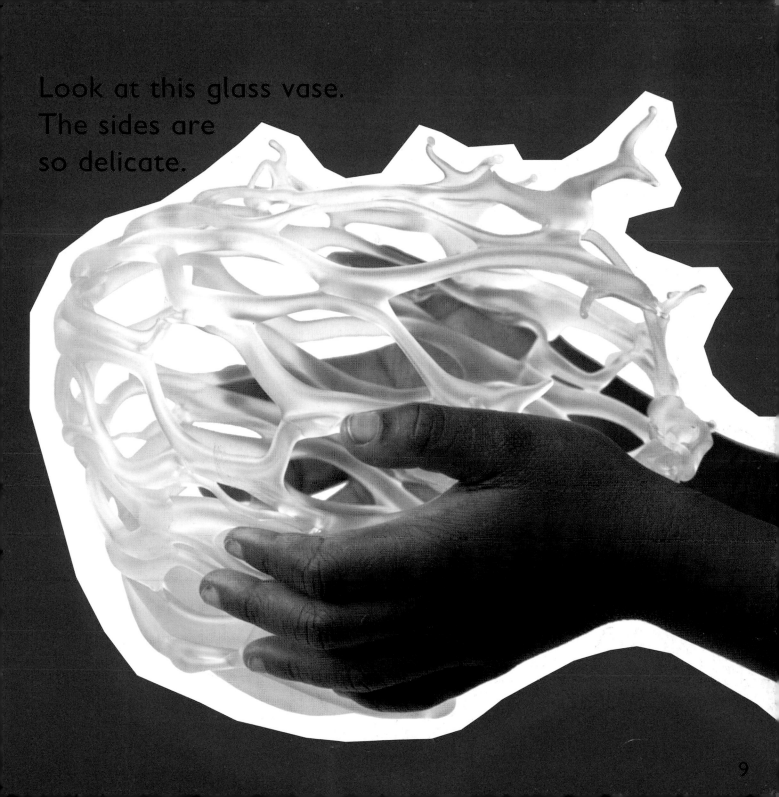

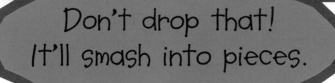

10

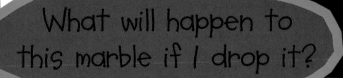

What will happen to this marble if I drop it?

It didn't smash.
I saw it bounce!

When glass is being made in a factory, it's very hot and soft.
It can be turned into lots of different shapes.

But something that's made
of glass doesn't change
its shape.

Unless it gets
broken or melted down
in a factory.

I've dropped some water
on to this piece of glass.

The water sits on top of the glass.
It doesn't soak through.

I wonder what will happen if I drop a marble into this tank of water.

This magnifying glass makes things look bigger.

I can see things better when I'm wearing my glasses.

Binoculars have magnifying glasses in them to make things look nearer.

In my Gran's garden there's a greenhouse made of glass. Gran grows tomato plants and flowers in it.

In the summer,
Gran lets me pick
the tomatoes.

It feels hot
inside the greenhouse.
It's more comfortable
in the fresh air.

Glass can be beautiful.
Look at this glass
ornament. It has
been made to look
like a shell.

There are so many colours in this paperweight. I can see blue, green, black and white.

Time to tidy away.

Let's sort these out into clear, green and brown glass for the bottle bank.

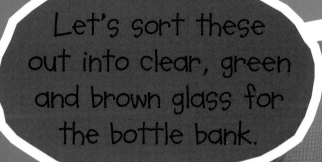

We've collected all these bottles and jars for recycling.

The glass can be taken back to a factory to be melted down and used again.

Notes for parents and teachers

The aim of the *Science Explorers* series is to introduce children to ways of observing and classifying materials, so that they can discover the various properties which make them suitable for a range of uses. By talking about what they already know about materials from their everyday use of different objects, the children will gain confidence in making predictions about how a material will behave in different circumstances. Through their explorations, the children will be able to try out their ideas in a fair test.

pp2/3, 4/5, 12/13

Glass is cheap to make from a mixture of (mostly) sand, soda ash and limestone with scrap glass (called cullet) added and heated in a furnace. Molten glass can be manipulated into a range of forms, from sheets of 'float glass' used for windows, to the threads of glass, finer than a single human hair, which are used in the telecommunications industry.

Ask the children to think of everyday things which are made from glass. How would those things be different if they were made from other materials? You could take the children on a 'materials walk', linking the uses of different materials to their various properties.

Introduce the children to objects they may not have thought of as having glass components, such as jewellery, cameras, mirrors, telescopes, computers and televisions and fibreglass canoes, fishing rods and crash helmets.

pp6/11

Provide the children with a range of objects which are made of, or which contain glass, stressing the importance of careful handling. Ask the children to describe how the glass objects look and feel. Record their responses and discuss them. Were any descriptive words used more than others?

Have the children ever seen broken glass at home, or on the street? Discuss how best to respond safely in a situation when glass is broken.

You could talk about the amazing contrasting properties of glass. Toughened glass can be made strong enough to be bullet-proof and glass can be made so thin and fragile that it is capable of being shattered by the sound of a sustained, high-pitched note.

pp14/15

Glass is particularly useful for kitchen (and laboratory) equipment because it is easy to keep clean, it doesn't deteriorate and it resists contamination.

The children's experiments with glass objects and water also provide an opportunity for them to begin to explore capacity. Ask them to compare different-shaped jars and bottles; which will hold the most water? How will they measure the amounts fairly? The children could record their results.

pp16/17

Glass can be ground and polished to make curved surfaces called lenses. Lenses bend light to make objects appear clearer or larger to the eye.

The children could go on a 'nature walk', exploring how magnifying lenses allow them to see things in more detail. Make sure that the children are aware that they should never look directly at the Sun with the naked eye, let alone through any lens.

pp18/19

Have any of the children been inside a greenhouse? Discuss (and if possible visit) the huge greenhouses which are used in garden centres and botanical gardens to cultivate plants in re-creations of tropical temperatures.

pp20/21

The plasticity of glass when it's hot means it can be made into beautiful sculptures and ornaments. Some glass sculptures may perform a function (e.g. as tables and chairs) as well being works of art.

The National Glass Centre in Sunderland (0191 515 5555) houses exhibitions covering the history of glass-making to the present day as well as studios with glassmakers giving demonstrations of their work.

pp22/23

Discuss the importance of recycling glass with the children and if possible, take them to see a bottle bank, making a collection of recyclable bottles and glass containers before you go. Why do they think the bottle bank is divided into clear, green and brown glass?

Find the page

Here is a list of some of the words and ideas in this book